Caring for Your Magical Pets

Taking care of Your Sea Monster

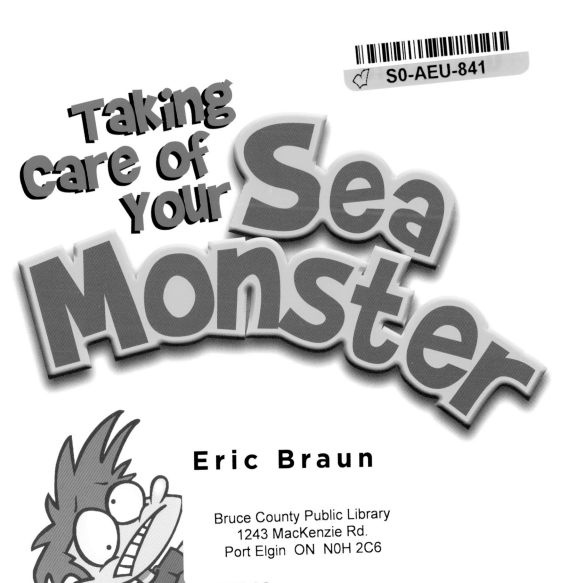

Eric Braun

BLACK
RABBIT
BOOKS

WA

Hi Jinx is published by Black Rabbit Books
P.O. Box 3263, Mankato, Minnesota, 56002.
www.blackrabbitbooks.com
Copyright © 2020 Black Rabbit Books

Marysa Storm, editor; Michael Sellner, designer;
Omay Ayres, photo researcher

Library of Congress Cataloging-in-Publication Data
Names: Braun, Eric, 1971- author, illustrator.
Title: Taking care of your sea monster / by Eric Braun.
Description: Mankato, Minnesota : Black Rabbit Books, [2020] |
Summary: Provides easy-to-read instructions for choosing and caring for
a pet sea monster, such as the challenge of learning to understand their
various noises. Includes discussion questions. | Includes bibliographical
references and index.
Identifiers: LCCN 2018042264 (print) | LCCN 2018052541 (ebook) |
ISBN 9781680729207 (e-book) | ISBN 9781680729146 (library binding) |
ISBN 9781644660935 (paperback)
Subjects: | CYAC: Sea monsters–Fiction. | Pets–Fiction.
Classification: LCC PZ7.1.B751542 (ebook) | LCC PZ7.1.B751542 Tas 2020
(print) | DDC [E]-dc23
LC record available at https://lccn.loc.gov/2018042264

Printed in China. 1/19

Image Credits

Alamy: Andrew Pearson, 20 (shark); Jerry LoFaro / Stocktrek Images, 11 (monster);
Oleg Saenco, 16 (dirty water); Dreamstime: Cory Thoman, 14 (fish), 15 (fish);
Inspirationupload, 12 (btm monster); Yael Weiss, Cover (top fish); iStock:
9lle, 8 (right); davidnay, 8 (btm); orensila, 12 (tank); Shutterstock:
Artem Maglyak, Cover (bkgd), 19 (bkgd); Blue Ring Media,
17 (handle); brgfx, 17 (wagon); designer_an, Back Cover
(bkgd), 3 (bkgd), 21 (bkgd); Daniel Eskridge, 6–7 (bkgd);
Dualororua, 16 (sponge, suds); hermandesign2015, 17
(boy, mud); kominque, 8 (top); Lyudmyla Kharlamova,
Cover (tube), 19 (tube); manas_ko, 16 (diver);
Memo Angeles, Cover (monster, boy), 6, 7, 14–15,
15, 18–19 (monster, boy); MicroOne, 11 (water);
Natutik, 4 (water); ne2pi, 2–3; nelya43, 14–15
(bkgd); Nearbirds, 12 (btm bkgd); Nihongo, 21
(monster); opicobello, 10; Pasko Maksim, Back
Cover (tear), 7 (tear), 23 (tear), 24; pitju, 9, 16
(page curl), 21 (page curl); Ron Dale, 5 (marker
stroke), 6 (marker stroke), 13, 20 (marker
stroke); Ron Leishman, 1, 11 (ladders, kids),
23 (btm); Sararoom Design, 4 (purple fish);
Sentavio, 12 (houses); totallypic, 20 (arrow);
VectorShots, 4 (shrimp), 5 (tadpole), 16
(tadpoles); your, 11 (clouds); Yusak_P, Cover
(bubbles), 18–19 (bubbles); zooco, 4 (monster)
Every effort has been made to contact copyright
holders for material reproduced in this book.
Any omissions will be rectified in subsequent
printings if notice is given to the publisher.

Contents

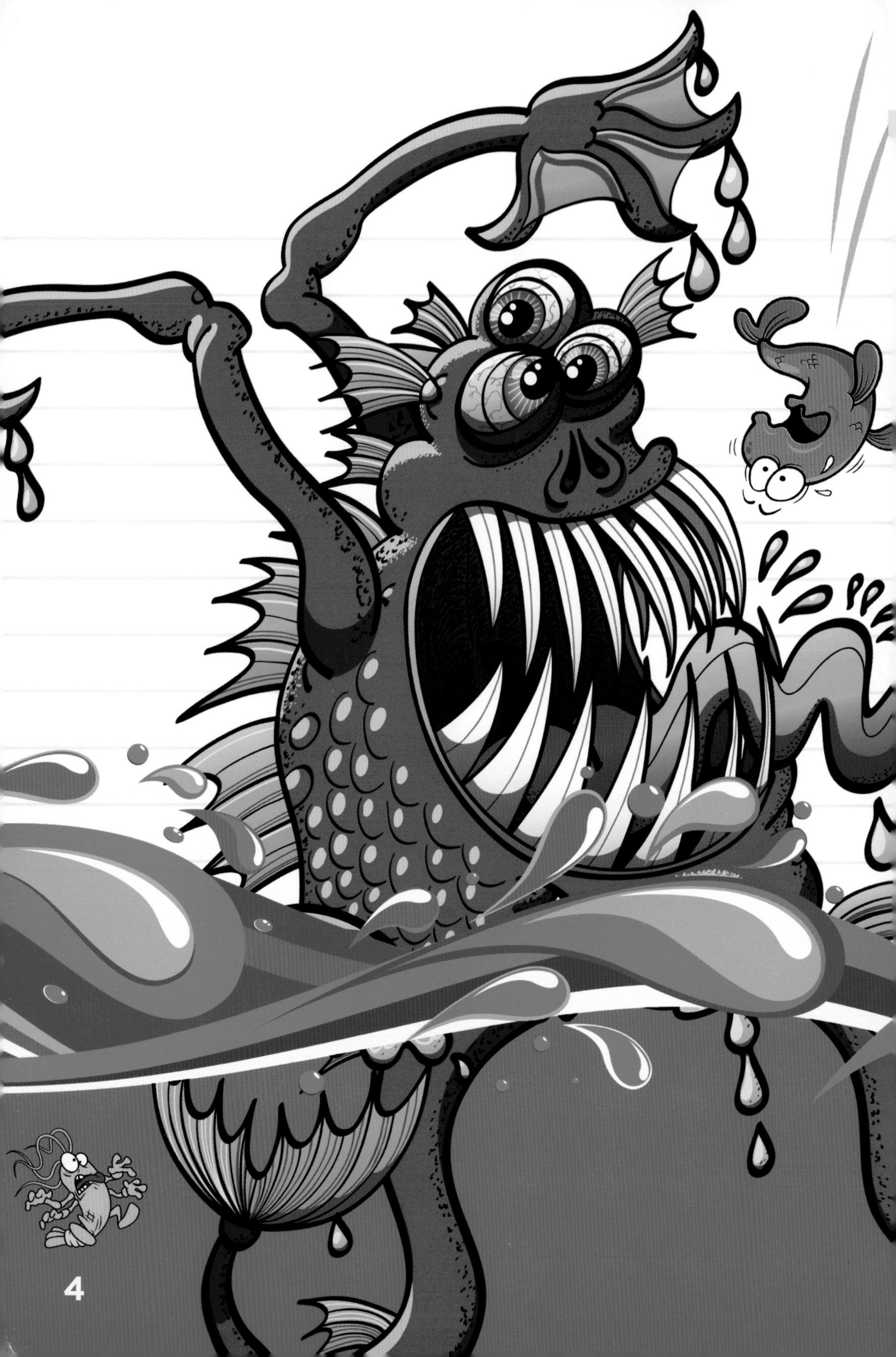

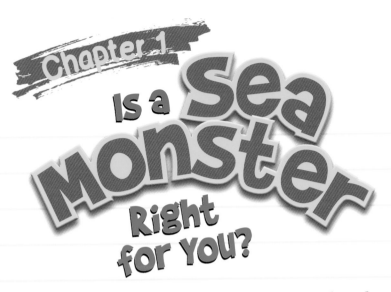

Chapter 1
Is a Sea Monster Right for You?

A sea monster rises from the depths. Its **tentacles** slap the water as it **chirps** in excitement. It's feeding time, and delicious fish are on the menu.

Sea monsters of the past destroyed cities and sank boats. Today, they make wonderful pets. The anger has been **bred** out of them, and they're quite sweet. There's still many challenges to owning one, though! A sea monster isn't for everyone.

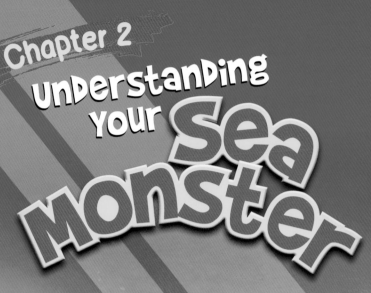

Chapter 2
Understanding your Sea Monster

There's a lot you must know before bringing home a sea monster. For starters, there are two main types. Reptilelike monsters look like dinosaurs.

Avoid buying your sea monster from a breeder. Instead, check local sea monster shelters. There are many sweet sea monsters waiting to be adopted.

Giant squidlike monsters, such as a kraken, have tentacles. These monsters are often harder to care for. Their many tentacles make it easy for them to cause trouble.

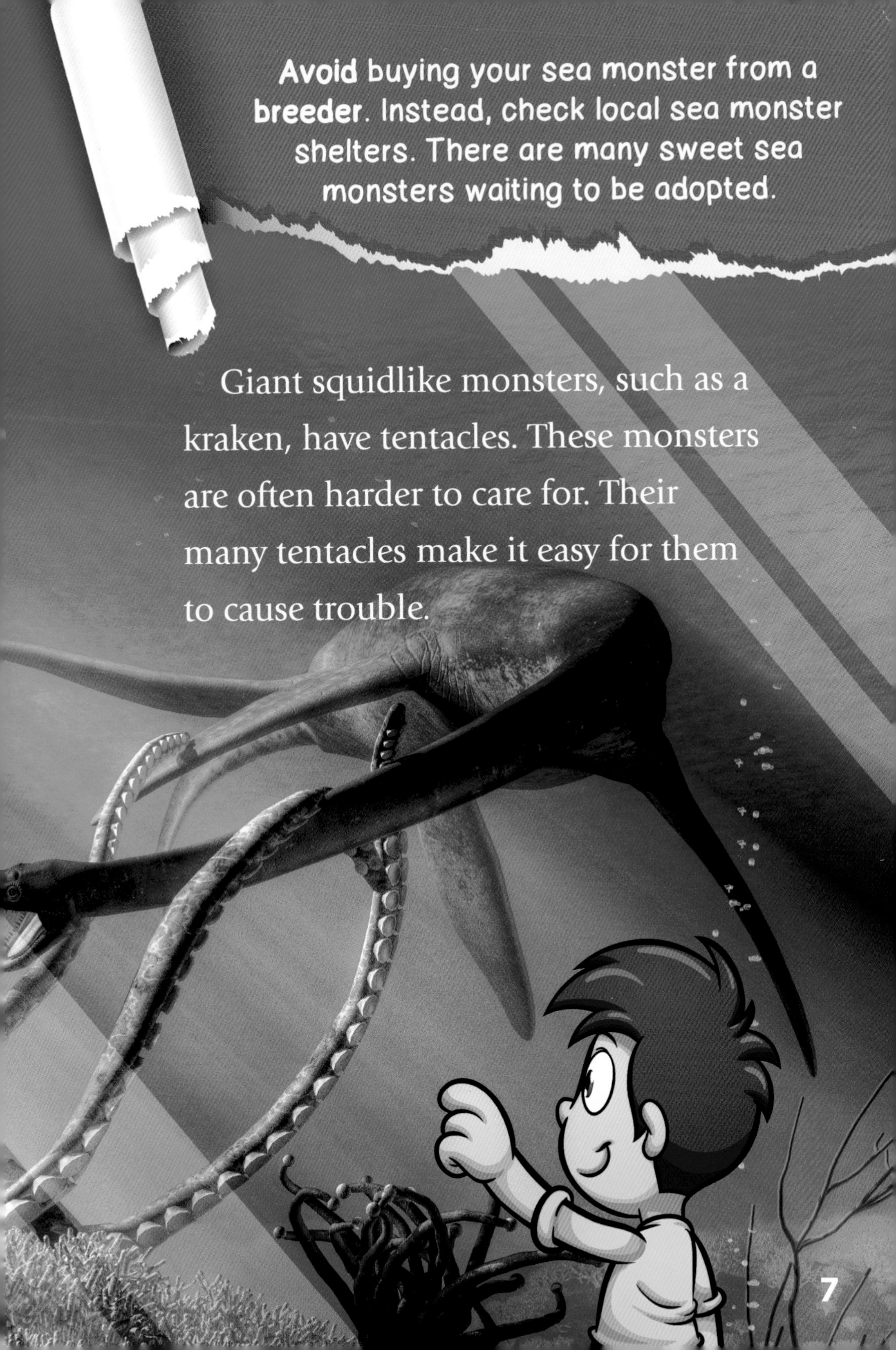

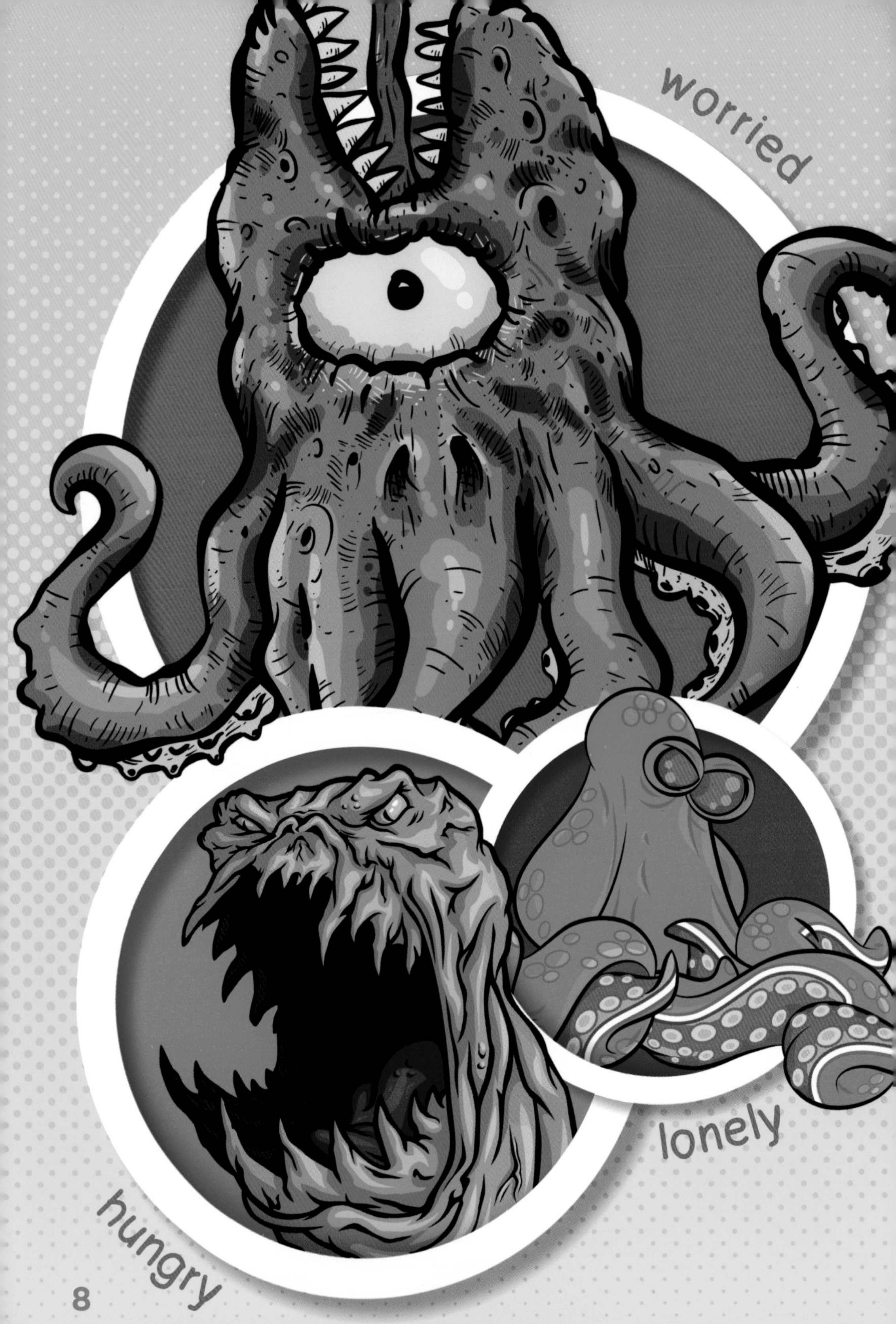
worried
lonely
hungry

Communication

One big part of understanding your sea monster is learning its noises. To **communicate**, they make a variety of sounds. Short, squeaky bursts mean they're worried. Lower grunts mean they are hungry. (These sounds might shake your walls!) Long, sad wails mean they're lonely. And chirps are sounds of joy.

Strong Bonds

Sea monsters like company. Yours will need attention and love. Call your monster to the surface of its tank. That's when you can pet it. Give it treats. But don't fall into the water! Sea monsters have poor eyesight. Your pet might think you're food!

Most sea monsters don't know their own strength. They might splash too much if they get excited. Be sure to train your monster.

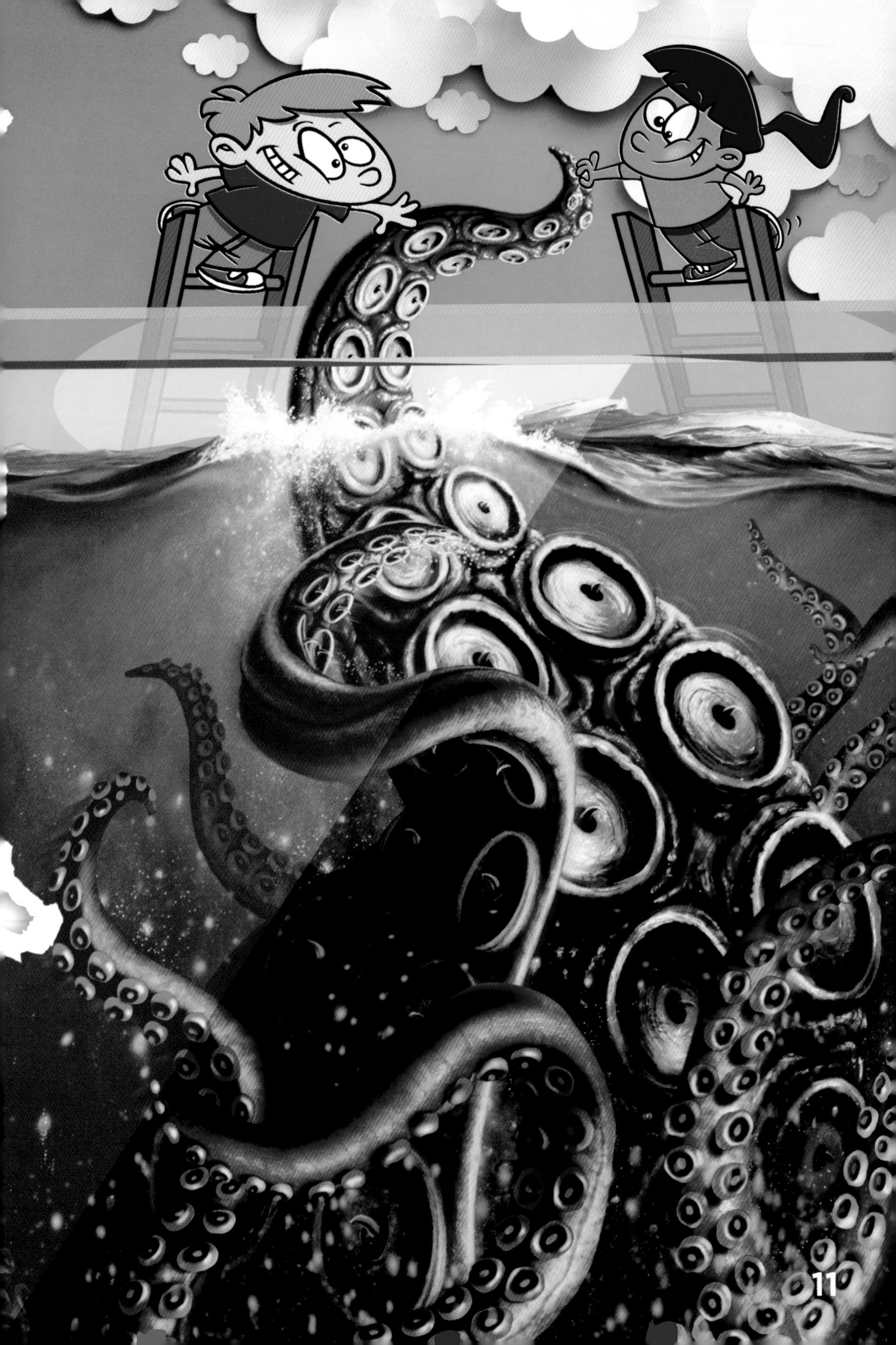

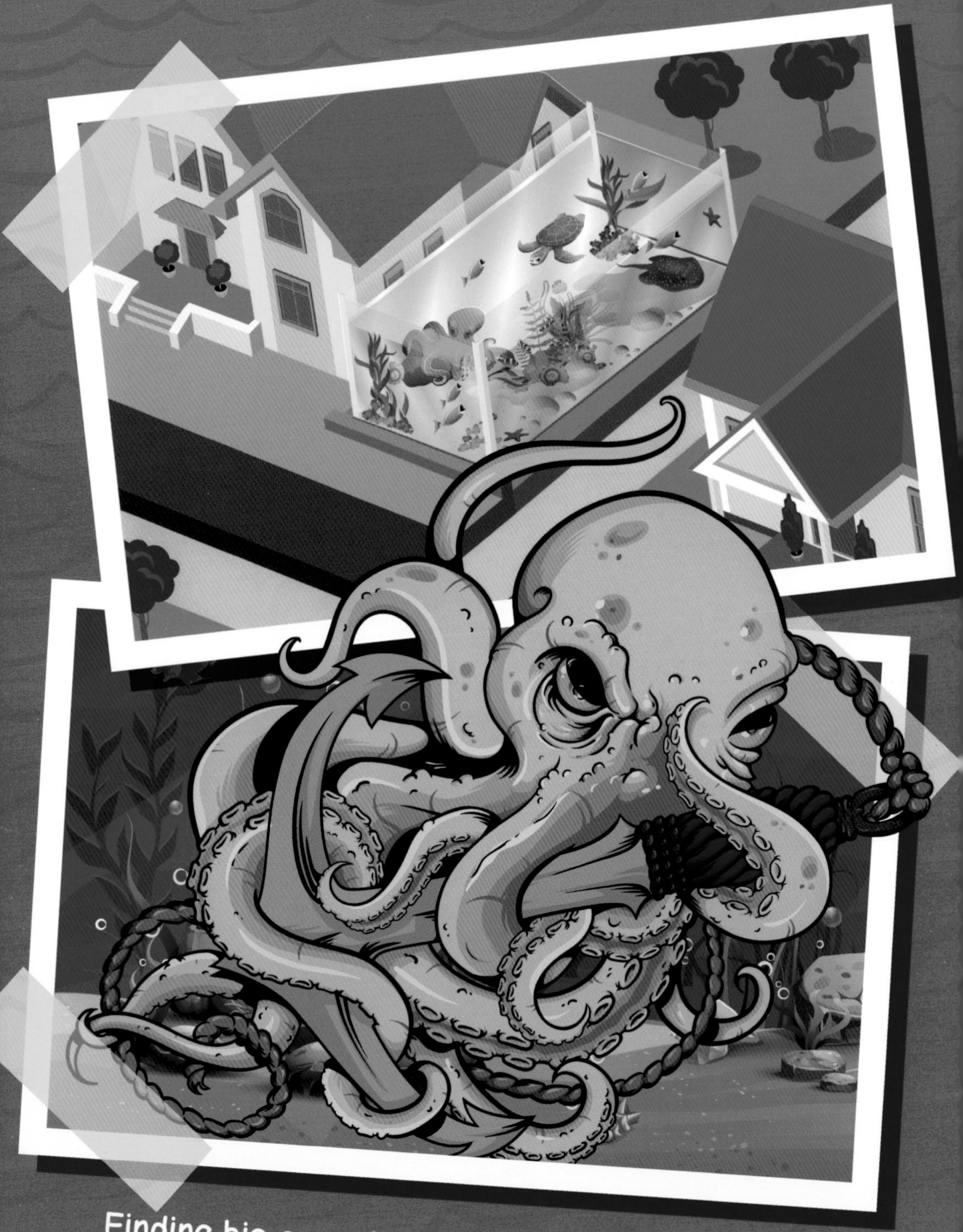

Finding big enough toys for your sea monster might be hard. Try sinking a full-sized ship in the tank. Your monster will have fun playing with it.

Chapter 3
Caring for Your Sea Monster

Caring for a sea monster isn't easy. First of all, it takes A LOT of space. Sea monsters need tanks the size of at least half a city block.

Having a big enough tank is only half the battle, though. You need to make sure it's full of the right kind of water. Some monsters live in salt water. Others need fresh water. The tank will need plenty of toys and hiding places too. Include rocky areas for the monster to rub against.

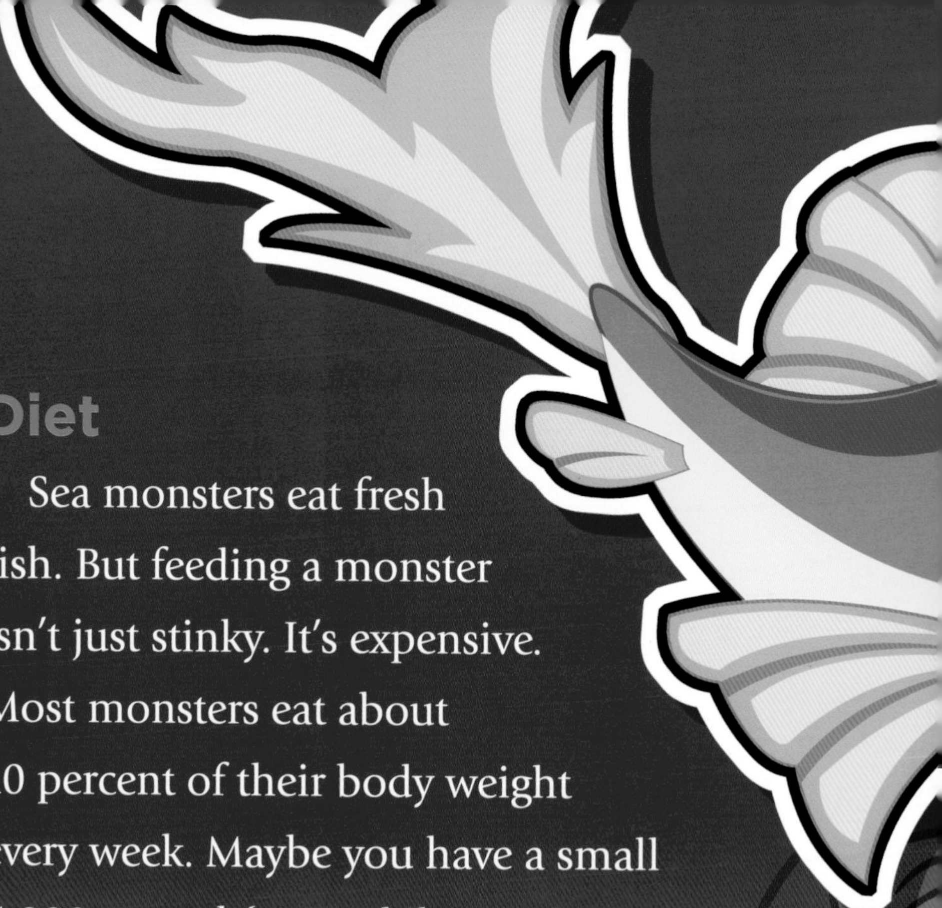

Diet

Sea monsters eat fresh fish. But feeding a monster isn't just stinky. It's expensive. Most monsters eat about 10 percent of their body weight every week. Maybe you have a small 5,000-pound (2,268-kilogram) monster. It only needs 500 pounds (227 kg) of fish each week. The bigger your monster, the more food it'll need.

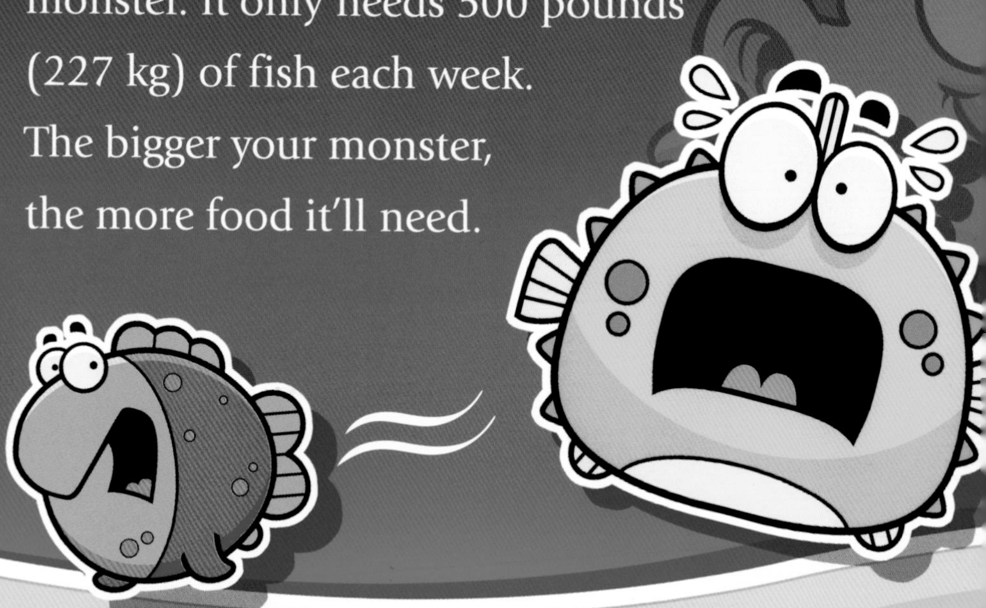

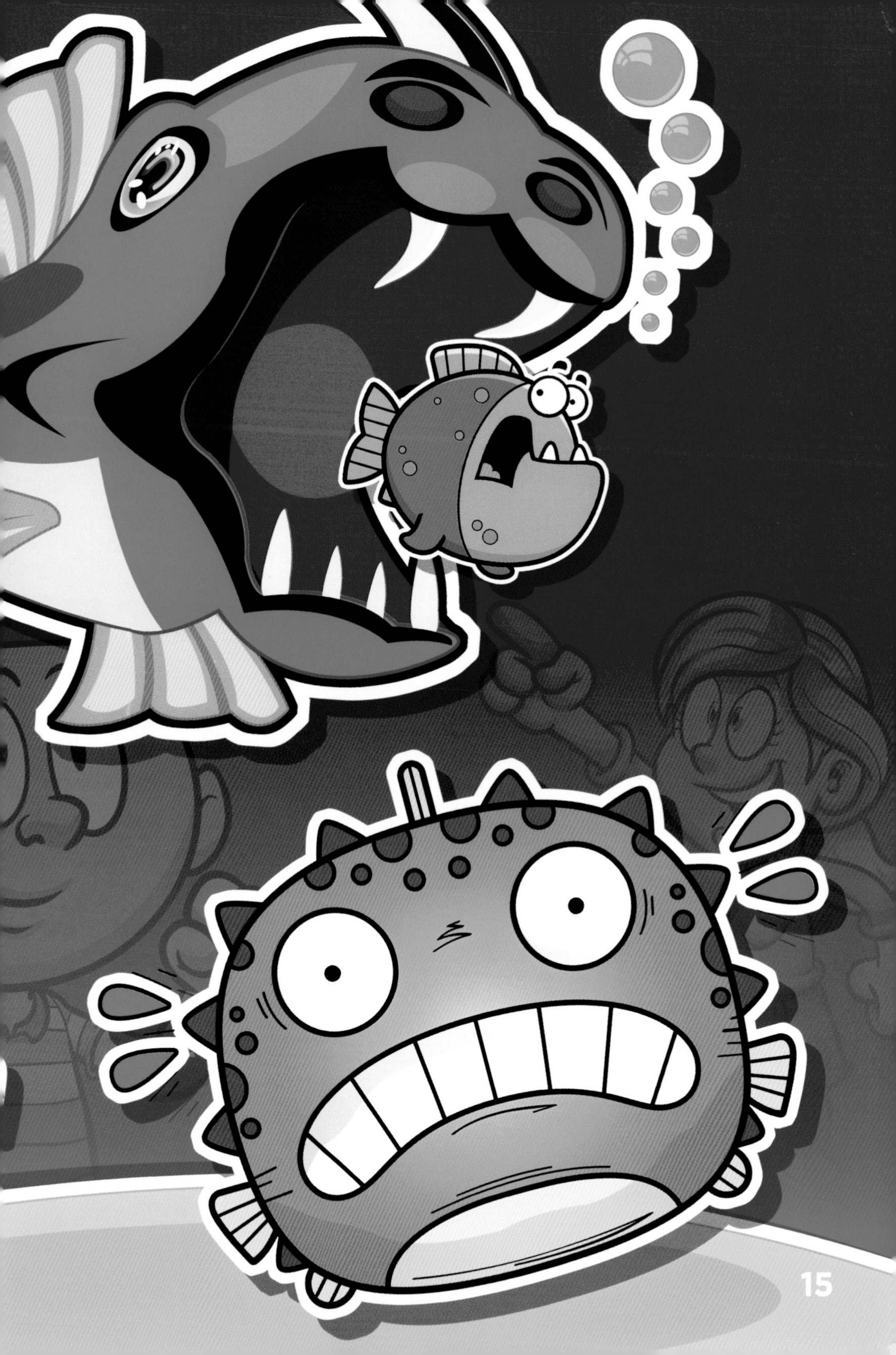

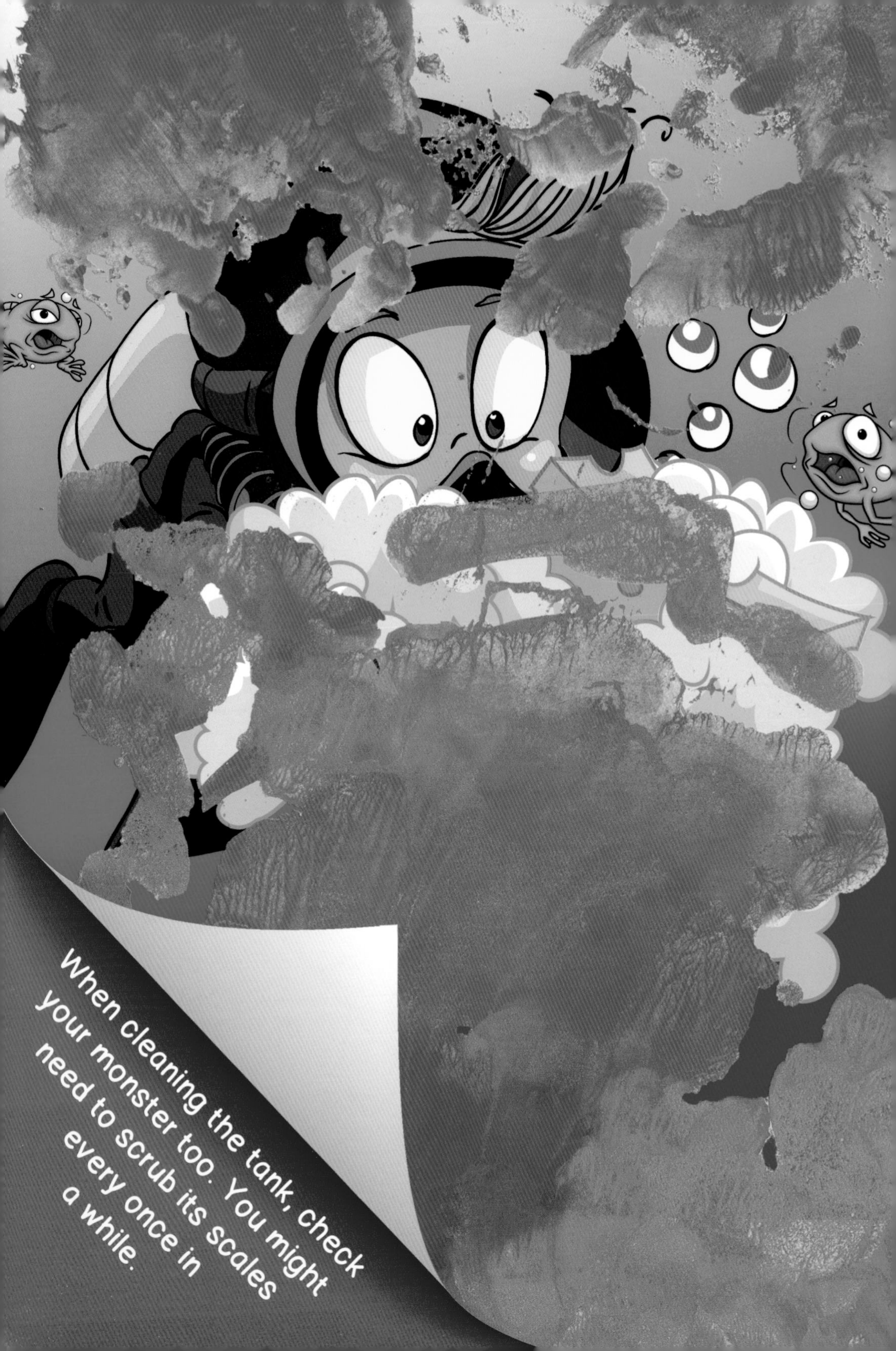

When cleaning the tank, check your monster too. You might need to scrub its scales every once in a while.

Tank Care

Sea monsters don't require much grooming. Their tanks, on the other hand, need regular cleaning. That's because sea monster poop really builds up. About once a month you'll have to clean the tank. First, you'll have to use a giant crane to remove your pet. Then you'll have to climb in and scrub every inch. Use a stiff brush and gentle soap. (Get a friend to help. It'll be fun!)

A Lifelong Friend

Caring for a sea monster takes time and money. It can be pretty dangerous too. But sea monster owners say it's worth the effort. Just remember to be good to your sea monster. It will reward you with love and happy memories.

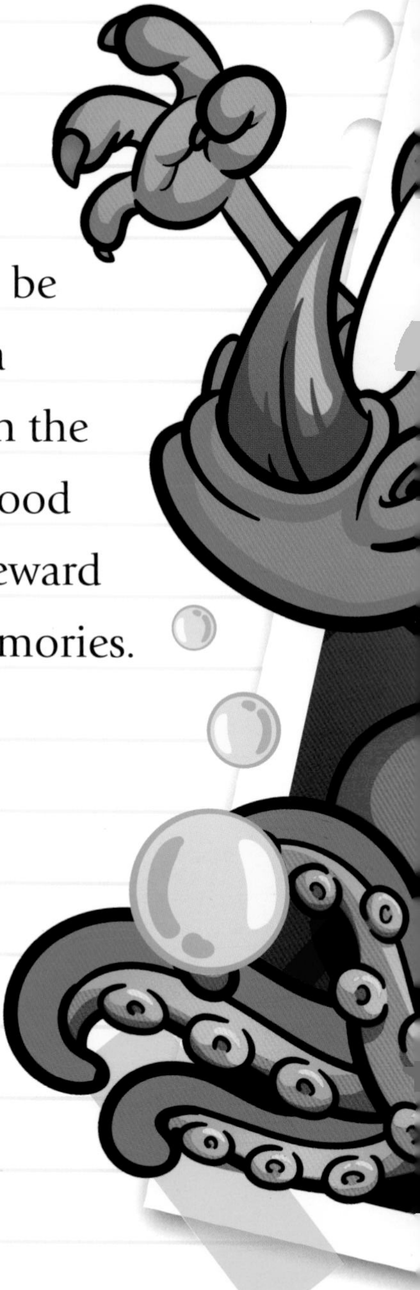

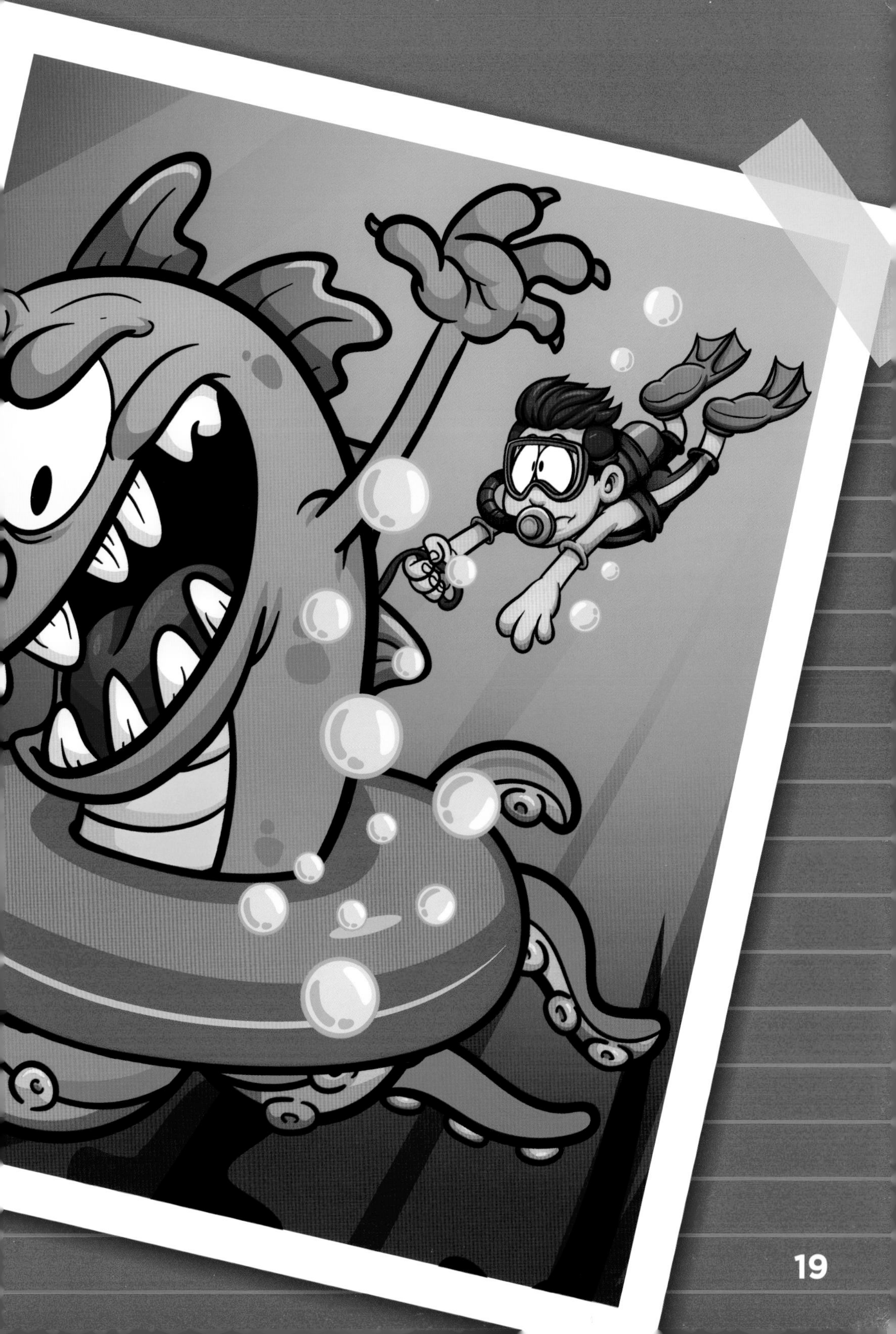

Chapter 4
Get in on the
Hi Jinx

Stories about sea monsters have been told for hundreds of years. They probably started when dead **deep-sea** creatures washed up on shore. People who found these creatures didn't know what they were. So the people made up stories to explain them. Giant squids led to stories about krakens. Mysterious **basking sharks** became sea **serpents**. As people shared the stories, the monsters got bigger and bigger.

Take It One Step More

1. Many people enjoy books and movies about sea monsters. Why do you think that is?

2. Do you think such a large animal would like living as a pet? Why or why not?

3. Make up your own sea monster. Where does it live? What does it look like?

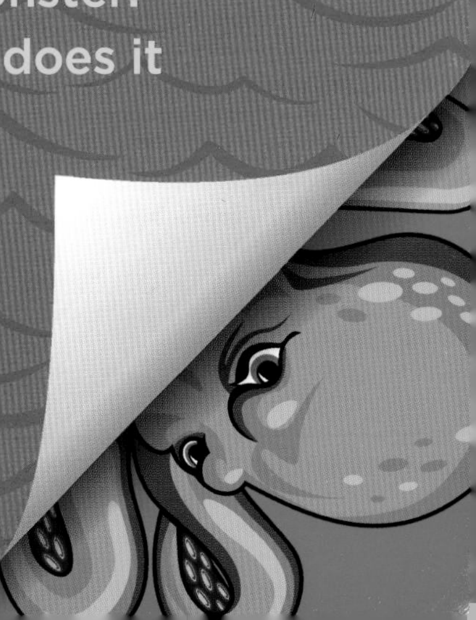

GLOSSARY

avoid (uh-VOYD)—to keep away from

basking shark (BAHSK-ing SHAHRK)—a large plankton-feeding shark that can grow up to 45 feet (14 meters) long

breed (BREED)—having two specific animals mate to create young with certain characteristics

breeder (BREE-der)—a person who raises animals with specific characteristics

chirp (CHURP)—to make a short high-pitched sound

communicate (kuh-MYU-nuh-kayt)—to share information, thoughts, or feelings so they are understood

deep-sea (DEEP-SEE)—living in, relating to, or done in the deep parts of the ocean

serpent (SUR-puhnt)—an usually large snake

tentacle (TEN-tuh-kuhl)—a long, flexible arm

LEARN MORE

BOOKS

Goddu, Krystyna Poray. *Sea Monsters: From Kraken to Nessie.* Monster Mania. Minneapolis: Lerner Publications, 2017.

Karst, Ken. *Sea Monsters.* Enduring Mysteries. Mankato, MN: Creative Education, 2018.

Loh-Hagan, Virginia. *Kraken.* Magic, Myth, and Mystery. Ann Arbor, MI: Cherry Lake Publishing, 2017.

WEBSITES

Sea Monster Facts
www.bbc.co.uk/sn/prehistoric_life/dinosaurs/seamonsters/

Sea Serpent
kids.britannica.com/kids/article/seaserpent/390052

Wacky Weekend: Freaky Sea Creatures
kids.nationalgeographic.com/explore/wacky-weekend/freaky-sea-creatures/#ww-sea-creatures-warty-frogfish.jpg

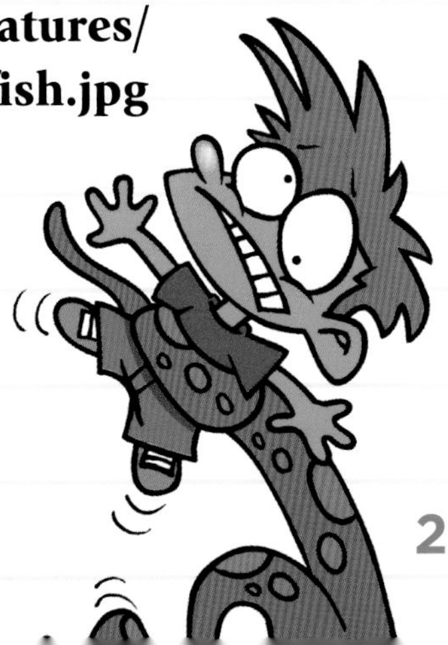

INDEX